I Love to Cuddle

I Love to Cuddle

Carl Norac ♥ Illustrated by Claude K. Dubois

DELL DRAGONFLY BOOKS  NEW YORK

Today Lola's mommy and daddy had to go out for a little while.
Before leaving, Mommy gave Lola a special cuddle.

"If you need anything," whispered Daddy, "Ms. Dumond is right outside in the garden. We'll be back very soon."

But right after Mommy and Daddy closed the door,
Lola was already lonely. *There's nobody here to give me a cuddle,*
she thought. *And I won't have fun with Ms. Dumond.*

Lola watched TV for a while,
but in the cartoons, no one ever thought of cuddling.

What can I do? wondered Lola.
I won't sulk or cry, because there's nobody here to see me.

Suddenly Lola had an idea:
*I'll bring every soft thing I can find
and make my very own Cuddle Island.*

My blanket and pillow are soft, she thought.

Brooms and buckets aren't soft at all!

Toilet paper is soft.

But not pots and pans.

In the kitchen, everything felt sticky.
There was nothing soft there.

But the bath towels were perfect.
Fluffy and cuddly.

This trash is smelly and not one bit soft, thought Lola.

My pink dinosaur has an ugly face,
but he's nice and soft!

"What's going on?" exclaimed Mommy.
"Where's Lola?" asked Daddy.

In the middle of all the mess,
they finally noticed a furry ball, fast asleep.

"Welcome to my lovely Cuddle Island!" shouted Lola as she woke up.

Mommy and Daddy told Lola to clean up the mess she'd made.
It was hard putting everything away, and it was taking so long!

Soon Mommy and Daddy joined Lola.
"We'll help you," they said.

"Now I don't have my Cuddle Island anymore," said Lola.
"But you've got us to cuddle with, sweetheart."

That night Lola couldn't fall asleep.
Her bed wasn't soft or warm enough.

Then she had a new idea.
On tiptoe, she slid silently out of her bedroom . . .

Tonight this will be my Cuddle Island!

For Sann and Hugo   For Apolline
—C.N.   —C.K.D.

Published by
Dell Dragonfly Books
an imprint of
Random House Children's Books
a division of Random House, Inc.
1540 Broadway
New York, New York 10036

Visit us on the Web! www.randomhouse.com/kids

Educators and librarians, for a variety of teaching tools, visit us at www.randomhouse.com/teachers

Library of Congress Cataloging-in-Publication Data
Norac, Carl.
I love to cuddle / by Carl Norac ; illustrated by Claude K. Dubois.
p. cm.
Summary: Lola the hamster is lonely when her parents go out, so she builds an island of soft, snuggly things to make herself feel better.
ISBN: 0-385-32646-7 (trade)
0-440-41741-4 (pbk.)
1. Hamsters—Fiction. 2. Loneliness—Fiction. I. Dubois, Claude K., ill. II. Title.
PZ7.N775115 Ial   1999
[E]—dc21   98-025646
CIP

Reprinted by arrangement with Doubleday Books for Young Readers

Printed in the United States of America

December 2002

10 9 8 7 6 5 4 3 2 1